For the fearless Marlows:
Theo, Tegan, Billie, Alex, Guy, Milo
– L. M.

For Pruno, whose amazing stories would
scare away our childhood fears.
– J. D.

LITTLE TIGER PRESS
1 The Coda Centre, 189 Munster Road, London SW6 6AW
www.littletiger.co.uk
First published in Great Britain 2005
This edition published 2013

The Witch With a Twitch

by Layn Marlow

Illustrated by Joëlle Dreidemy

Kitch was an ordinary witch's cat.
    But his beloved mistress, Willa, was
no ordinary witch.

The rest of the witches called her cowardly custard, and even Kitch had to admit his witch was a bit of a scaredycat.

Toads made her tremble,

Yikes!

nighttime made her nervous,

Shiver!

and spiders made her jump out of her skin!

Screech!

Willa was a very twitchy witch, which could only spell trouble for Kitch.

One dark night, Willa and Kitch were zooming through the sky on their broom.

Willa was already feeling twitchy in the darkness, when suddenly . . .

Oh no! An owl!
What a fright!
The witch twitched,
the broomstick pitched,

Aaaah!

and Kitch ended up in the mud!

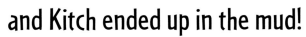

Splat!

Poor Kitch!

Willa took him home for a special bath. Using two drops of magic potion, she began a spell to make Kitch's fur shiny and sleek again. Drip, drip. But suddenly . . .

Oh no! A mouse!
What a terror!
The witch twitched,
the spell switched,

Squeak!
Squeak!

and Kitch found himself
covered in spots!
He looked ridiculous.

Poor spotted Kitch!

He spent the night trying to hide. But he was soon discovered by the other cats. They teased Kitch until he couldn't stand it anymore.

LOST
SWEETY

please call
555-0123

MEGA
SHOE

He made up his mind
to run away to the sea.

Dear Willa,
gone to be a
ship's cat.

Meanwhile, Willa searched all night for the spell to cure Kitch.

Finally, she found it and hurried to help her spotted cat.

But all she spotted was his note.
Willa was very upset. Kitch was gone!
She had to find him!

Willa searched high and low,

but she couldn't find Kitch anywhere . . .

until at last, she saw a tiny boat being
tossed around on the stormy sea.

On the deck was a sickly looking Kitch.
He was overjoyed to see Willa again!

The witch raised her wand to cast a
calming spell on the water, but suddenly . . .

a gigantic
WHALE rose out of the ocean!
What a shock!

The boat dipped
and Kitch slipped—
right into the deep, cold water!
SPLASH
He had never been so afraid.
Kitch was in real danger!

Without the slightest twitch,
Willa dodged the whale,

braved the waves,

and hauled her
dear cat to safety.

Back home, Willa magicked the spots away and fussed over her cat until he felt better.

Now Willa didn't give two hoots about swooping owls, or snooping mice, or even scary spiders! Kitch was safe and sound and very proud of his own dear, kind, BRAVE witch.

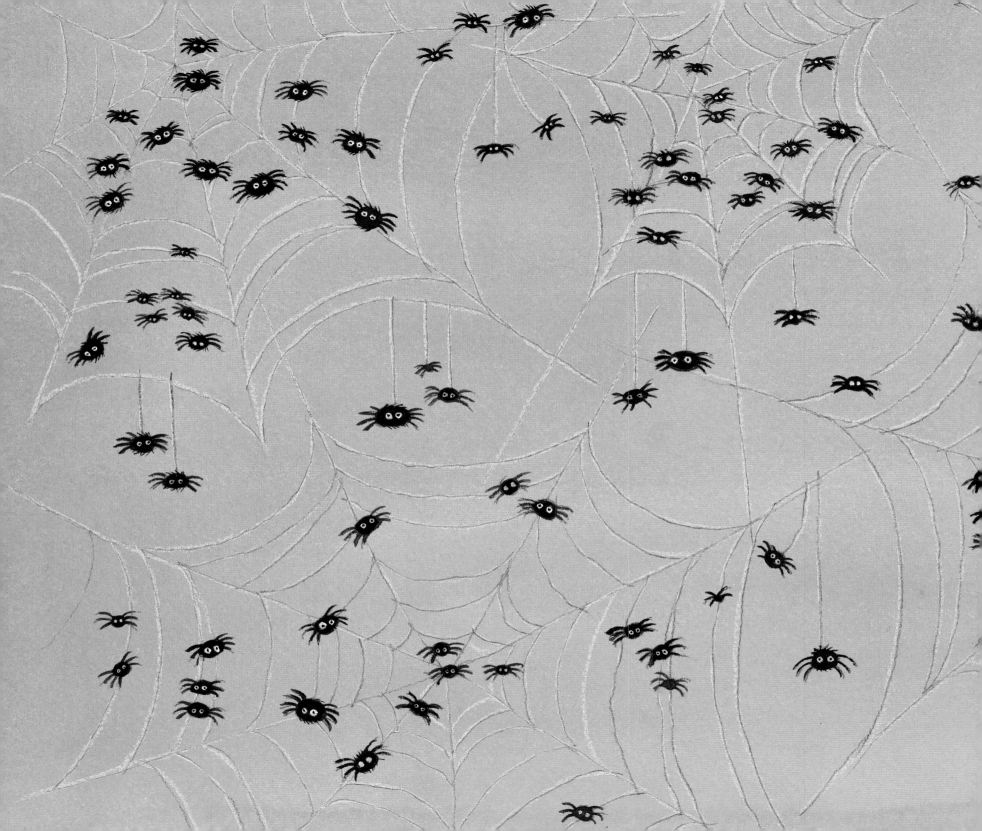